Inside the Animal Kingdom

Ugochukwu Ikwuakor

To: Uzoma

May God bless!

VANTAGE PRESS
New York

Illustrated by Tanya Stewart

FIRST EDITION

Copyright © 2005 by Ugochukwu Ikwuakor

Published by Vantage Press, Inc.
419 Park Ave. South, New York, NY 10016

Manufactured in the United States of America
ISBN: 0-533-14881-2

Library of Congress Catalog Card No.: 2004091512

0 9 8 7 6 5 4 3 2

To Uzoma, Kelechi, and Uchenna, for their prayers and contributions. To Tina, for her spiritual advice. To Professor Trish Max of Marymount Manhattan College, for her wonderful lectures and guidance. To Chief Abdulaziz and Dr. Philomena Ude for their kindness.

Contents

Minding Your Own Business: The Turtle and the Squirrel

(Why Turtle Has a Checkered Shell)

In everyday life, some people tend to go about their business quietly and without publicity, sometimes mainly for their own safety and the safety of their families.

Once upon a time there was a great famine in the animal kingdom. There was no rain and no farming for three years. The animals, both young and old, were dying of hunger, except for Squirrel. When the situation became too much to bear, all the animals decided to call a meeting. They wanted to appease the gods of their land to save them from their trouble.

During the meeting, which was held on a market day, suggestions were made on what to do about the famine and on how to appease the gods. Looking around, they saw Squirrel looking healthy and agile, and his coat was as shiny as gold and silver. He looked very

different from the other animals. Dog sighed and looked dejected.

"We have not seen you and your family around lately," Dog said. "I believe you are now living in a better place."

"Why are you not feeling the hunger like every other animal?" Sheep asked Squirrel.

"My ancestors are taking good care of me and my family," Squirrel replied.

"Oh yeah? I have ancestors, too, but look at me," said Cat.

"Me too," said Cow.

The animals did not believe him, but what could they do? Nothing.

The true fact was that Squirrel, while living and working together with other animals, also had a home in the sky where he had sent his family to stay during the great famine. In the sky they ate golden apples from the trees, and gathered and stored the food. Turtle, well respected for his wisdom and cunning, was also not satisfied with the answer Squirrel gave the animals.

The next day, Turtle was on his way to see a friend when he saw Cow.

"How are you, wise one?" asked Cow.

"Not so good," replied Turtle. "I am hungry and I can't walk."

"I hardly give my kids enough milk," Cow said. "By the way, Turtle, what do you think about Squirrel?"

"I don't believe him and all that stuff about his ancestors," Turtle answered.

"Can you find out what he's been up to?" Cow requested.

"I surely will," said Turtle. "I think he is hiding something."

"Bye."

"Bye."

Turtle started following Squirrel around without Squirrel noticing. One day he followed Squirrel to his hideout. He watched and waited.

Squirrel, believing that he was alone and safe, called out to his mother in the sky to send down the rope to him. Immediately, a long rope was thrown down from the sky, and quickly, Squirrel climbed up and the rope disappeared. Turtle could not believe his eyes. He went home thinking about what he saw. The next day he followed Squirrel to the same spot and again the same thing happened. While this was going on, Squirrel did not suspect anything.

Then, on one special day, Turtle decided to surprise Squirrel and his family, or as he put it, "to pay them a visit." On that fateful day, Turtle went to Squirrel's hideout, and disguising his voice to sound like Squirrel's voice, he called out to Squirrel's mother.

"Throw down the rope," Turtle said in Squirrel's voice. The rope fell from the sky.

Unfortunately for Turtle, Squirrel was not in the sky but was down on Earth. He was climbing the rope sluggishly when at that point in time came Squirrel. He saw the rope and Turtle and knew something was wrong.

With a high voice, Squirrel called out to his mother, "Cut the rope." The rope was cut and Turtle fell to the ground. He landed with a thump! His shell broke in pieces. He cried and wailed in agony.

Animals passing by heard the cry and rushed through the woods and toward the voice. They saw Turtle twisting on the ground. Some animals tended to him while others went to get help. The doctors in the animal kingdom gathered the pieces of Turtle's shell and managed to save his life by piecing his shell together. And that is why Turtle now moves along in a checkered shell.

One Life to Live: The Hen and the Hare

(How Hen's Chickens Go to Heaven)

Some individuals view their personal lives as something extraordinary, their sufferings as something that never happened before, and their personal experiences as the worst things that ever happened.

One fine Sunday afternoon, Hen was going to visit her parents in Oki, a village six miles from Ebe, her own village. Suddenly, she saw Rabbit running fast without looking back, as if something was coming after him. Hen ran as fast as she could, but could not catch up with Rabbit. She was surprised to see Rabbit at that particular time of the day. It is believed that rabbits do not come out during the day, and if they are seen during the day, it is a bad omen.

Thinking of what might have happened, Hen decided to get to her parents' home early to find out what was wrong. She believed that

seeing Rabbit at that time of the day was bad luck. She became afraid that something bad had happened to her parents. Hen made her journey to Oki in good time, met her parents in good health, and was happy.

When Hen returned to her village, however, Ebe was not in order. She asked what had happened and was told that the only son of Hare had died. Hare had locked himself up and refused to eat or allow anyone to see him. He wanted to die and follow his dead son. Hearing the sad news, Hen realized why she saw the rabbit during the day. As should be known, Hare was the first cousin of Rabbit.

After resting for a while from her journey, Hen decided to go and see if she could convince Hare to come out from his prison and stop his hunger strike. She reached Hare's house. With a high voice she yelled out to Hare, "Get on with your life. You are a coward and silly and behaving badly."

Hen then told him a story about herself and said, "I would have been the greatest female on earth if it wasn't for my destiny. I once had seven beautiful chickens; two were hit by cars, another two were stolen by Falcon, and the birthday party took one. How many do you think remained?" she asked Hare.

"Two," Hare replied.

Hen continued. "On the day the medicine man meditated, one of my remaining chickens was given up for sacrifice, and the head of the household used the last chicken for the year's new-yam festival. From my story, you will realize that your life is not as bad as mine or worse than anyone else's. I am the bravest female on earth," she said. "So if you want to die, go ahead and die, but bear in mind that the world takes no notice of that, whether you live or not. Oh! One more thing, Hare, all my chickens are in heaven."

Hearing Hen's story, Hare felt he was making a fool of himself. He decided to stop his cowardly ways, and to continue living his own life just like Hen, no matter what happened.

The Taste of Injustice: The Horse, Leopard, and Cheetah

(How Cheetah and Horse Became Friends)

Good friends tend to help each other, and when friends become greedy toward one another, that friendship becomes worthless.

Once upon a time, Horse and Leopard were good friends. They were members of the same club in the animal kingdom, but were not from the same village. Horse's village was Abi and Leopard's village was Anam. But their villages had many things in common, such as sharing the same lake.

One day, Horse was in another village on a mission. He sent word to Leopard to buy him two pairs of new shoes. When he returned from his mission, Leopard gave him the shoes, but he did not have enough money to pay Leopard. An agreement was reached between the two on how Horse would pay the money.

When the money was fully paid, Leopard

13

demanded more money from Horse. Horse thought that Leopard was kidding and said, "No." Leopard insisted on getting the money from Horse. He told Horse that their agreement did not give him the right to own the shoes.

"Are you joking?" Horse asked his friend.

"Do I look like I am joking?" Leopard shot back. "I meant every word I said, whether you like it or not."

Before that incident, Horse had never had any personal dealings with Leopard and he was surprised to see his friend behave that way. "How could Leopard do such a thing?" Horse questioned. He decided to deal with Leopard in any way possible.

Members of Leopard's family heard what happened between Horse and Leopard and intervened. They begged Horse to give them a chance to look into it. Horse agreed and a day was set for them to meet. On the appointed day, both families met. Horse and Leopard were asked to state their cases. After a while, tension was high and Horse became angry. "You're lying," he said to Leopard.

Cheetah did not like his cousin Leopard being called a liar. "How dare you call him a liar!" Cheetah shouted at Horse. "He bought you the shoes with his own money and you are not grateful."

"Your cousin is a cheat, same as you!" Horse shouted back. Cheetah jumped at the horse for a fight. He was asked to behave himself and keep out of what did not concern him. Throughout the meeting Cheetah kept on making faces at Horse.

The meeting was not in Horse's favor and he lost the case. He was told that the shoes belonged to Leopard because there was no agreement that said otherwise. Horse did not believe it. "You are all a bunch of animals," he told them.

"What are you, then?" Cheetah interrupted and pointed his paw at Horse.

Horse kicked and raved, but the outcome of the meeting was no surprise to him. He had sensed it because most of those present were members of Leopard's family. Those in favor of Horse were small in number. He took what happened as "one of those things in life."

A few months after that meeting, Horse bought his own new pair of shoes, to the surprise of Leopard and his cousin, Cheetah. During that period, Cheetah received the same

injustice from his cousin, Leopard, that Horse had received.

It happened that Cheetah wanted a pair of gloves from Leopard. Leopard bought the gloves for him, but trouble started when Cheetah found out that the amount of money Leopard demanded from him was three times the cost of the gloves. The gloves were also not of good quality.

Cheetah refused to accept the gloves from Leopard. He then remembered what happened between Leopard and Horse and realized that he was wrong in attacking Horse some time ago for no reason. Since that time, Cheetah and Leopard have not been on good speaking terms and distanced themselves from each other. Cheetah went to Horse and apologized and they made up and became friends.

The Prize of Disobedience: The Bat and the Birds

(Why Bats Live on Trees and Roofs)

As the saying goes, "No one is indispensable." Nobody should brag about his or her wealth or power; they could be nothing or nobody tomorrow.

Once upon a time King Bird ruled the birds. He had wisdom and power. The first day of each month, the birds met at the palace to hear their king and to receive instructions. Each of the three villages in the bird kingdom was told what to do and how to do it. It was up to their leaders, Eagle, Falcon, and Bat, to see that everything got done.

In King Bird's army, both Eagle and Falcon were warriors, but Bat was higher in rank. The only reason for that was that Bat's village was greater in number than the other two villages combined, and because of that, Bat was very powerful.

As time went on, Bat started giving orders in and around his own village and took control of some areas of the kingdom without seeking advice from the king or asking the opinion of other leaders.

The king was told of Bat's behavior. Bat was invited to the palace to meet with the king, but he refused to go. King Bird sent personal invitations to Bat through his messengers, but Bat ignored the king's invitations. Once, he asked his guards to beat up the messengers and sent them back to the king. The king was very angry when he saw what Bat did to his messengers.

By then it appeared to the birds that Bat was up to something against the kingdom, and rumors started to spread that Bat was about to form his own army. During that time, Bat gave instructions that every member of his own village in the army must come back home. He wanted to create his own kingdom. A great number of birds left their positions in the kingdom and joined Bat's army.

The king called the leaders and elders of his kingdom, including Eagle and Falcon, to ask them what to do. The king did not want war. Before that meeting with the leaders and elders, the king sent more delegates to Bat to try to talk to him. Bat refused to listen. He sent the delegates back with no encouraging word to the king or to the elders.

While most of the birds in Bat's village supported him, others had mixed feelings about fighting their fellow birds. King Bird felt betrayed and decided he had no choice but to fight Bat. While this went on, Bat continued to rally his troops. The king met with his own army and gave out assignments. Eagle was chosen to lead the King's troops and Falcon became his second-in-command.

Bat's army went to war against the rest of the kingdom, which was led by Eagle. Bat didn't know that King Bird was very popular among the birds. The king on several occasions had saved the kingdom from danger. Bat's army was greater in number than Eagle's army, but with leadership and intelligence, Eagle defeated Bat in battle. When Eagle and his army moved in to arrest Bat, he flew away toward the animal kingdom.

The animals knew about the birds and the defeat of Bat, and when they heard he escaped and was flying to the animal kingdom, Lion King sent out his leaders to stop Bat from

landing. When Bat saw Elephant, Tiger, Dog, Pig, and others, he stopped short on a tree and greeted them. With his feet perched on the branch, Bat stretched himself down and extended his wings to the animals. They ignored him, and Elephant told him he was not invited to the animal kingdom. Bat pleaded, but without success. The animals left him on the tree and went home.

Bat felt rejected. He waited and hoped the animals would change their minds and invite him into their kingdom. When night set in, he became very tired and hungry, and he fell asleep. The next day, he continued to wait on the tree and hoped that the animals would be back to invite him in. They did not. Realizing he had nowhere to go, Bat decided to make the tree his home, and since that time, he has been living on trees and roofs.

The Time Keeper: The Rooster and His Fate

(Why Rooster Became the Timekeeper)

To be present during a meeting enables one to know the situation of things, and at the same time contribute to what is going on.

Once upon a time in the animal kingdom, Lion King announced that every animal must be at the Market Square to vote on who would be the official timekeeper for the kingdom. For hours after the announcement, there was confusion and anxiety among the animals. None of the animals wanted to be a timekeeper.

"Why do we need a timekeeper?" asked Pig.

"I don't know. Maybe to keep time during meetings," Bear said.

"But we have Dog, the provost," said Pig. "He can keep the time, too."

"Whoever wants to be the timekeeper, can be, but not I," said Cat.

"Nor I," said Bear.

"Nor I," said Pig.

On the appointed day, which fell on a market day, all the animals, except Rooster, gathered at the Market Square. Rooster was fond of taking things for granted and loved to jest away whenever there were serious issues to discuss. When Rooster heard about Lion King's announcement, he decided not to attend. "It is going to be one of those useless meetings," Rooster told his wife, Mina. "You can go and represent us."

"How do you know it is useless?" Mina asked. "You must attend."

"Not I," said Rooster.

"Nor I," said his wife.

Rooster and his wife did not attend the meeting at the Square. At noon on that day, Lion King arrived at the Square and was greeted with cheers.

A small section of the crowd murmured, but their voices were drowned by the large group clapping and shouting the name of their king. Dog, who also was the chief messenger in the animal kingdom, rang the big bell and every animal became quiet.

Lion King addressed the crowd and explained why they gathered. He asked them to vote and select their timekeeper. Some of the animals started to murmur again.

"Woof!" barked the dog. "Order!"

Everyone was quiet. Porcupine, who never liked to be ignored, raised her voice and spoke. "I nominate Rooster as the official timekeeper," she said. The animals looked around but did not see Rooster in the crowd.

A majority of the animals voted in favor of Rooster as the timekeeper.

Rooster did not blame anyone but himself for his fate, and since then, he has crowed to announce sunset and sundown.

One Good Turn Deserves Another: The Mouse and the Lion

(How Lion and Mouse Became Friends)

A friend in need is a friend forever. Those who show kindness to others usually get rewarded in life.

Once upon a time in the animal kingdom, the animals built a warehouse where they could store food for the winter months. All of the animals contributed food to the warehouse, but some of them, like the mouse, couldn't afford to do that. But each animal received extra food from the warehouse whether they contributed or not. All they had to do was ask.

"I am not going to beg for food," Mouse said to himself. "I am smart enough to find my own food and I have food to last me all winter."

Whatever food Mouse had, did not last him, and he was too proud to ask for food from the warehouse. The warehouse became

29

a source of relief during hard times in the kingdom and it lasted a long time. One morning, Bear was coming home from his early fishing when he saw the door of the warehouse open. He ran across the road to the warehouse shouting, "Someone broke into the warehouse! Someone broke into the warehouse!"

Other animals heard Bear's voice and ran toward the warehouse.

"Wait," said Deer. "Maybe King's maids are taking some food."

"This early in the morning?" Cat asked.

"It could be thieves," Toad said. "Let's go in and see."

They went into the warehouse and immediately Deer shouted, "It's Mouse! It's Mouse! He is stealing food!" Mouse saw the animals and ran to the door to get out, but they blocked his way. He ran back to the stack of food and they chased him. He jumped on top of a plank by the wall, bounced off the wall and landed on top of Bear's head. Bear yelled, "Get off me! Get off me," and fell on the floor. Mouse jumped down and ran back to the wall and to a tiny hole in the wall, but Cat outran

him and caught him. They took Mouse to the King.

Mouse was tried and found guilty of stealing. He was asked to pay a fine or go to jail, and was given time to pay it, but he could not. He was again brought to the palace to be sent to jail, but King's nephew (a lion named Odum), came to Mouse's rescue. Odum was well known as a friend of the poor. He paid the fine for Mouse and Mouse was set free. Mouse thanked Odum for his help.

Two years after that incident, Odum was going to his mother's village early one morning to visit his uncle, when he accidentally fell into a net-trap set by the hunters. The trap was covered and he did not see it. The hunters usually checked their traps in late afternoon. Odum was there for hours, and not knowing what to do, he resigned himself to fate. Suddenly, and from nowhere came Mouse, who was on his way to visit his cousin. Mouse saw Odum inside the trap and knew he was in trouble.

Wasting no time, Mouse cut the ropes, one after another, until Odum was set free. "Thank you so much for your kindness," Lion said to Mouse.

"This is nothing compared to what you did for me years ago," Mouse replied. "I learned not to be too proud." They again thanked each other and went their different ways—Lion, to his mother's village, and Mouse, to his cousin. Since then, Mouse and Lion have been friends.